This

READ with ME

Book

Belongs To

_____

For Leon Friedberg, my father.
He told the most beautiful story of all in silence.

Library of Congress Cataloging in Publication Data

Perle, Ruth Lerner.
   Sleeping beauty, with Benjy and Bubbles.
   (Read with me series)
   SUMMARY: A rhymed retelling of the classic tale with Benjy the bunny and Bubbles the cat.
   [1. Fairy tales.   2. Folklore—Germany.   3. Stories in rhyme]   I. Maestro, Giulio.   III. Title.   IV. Series.
                  PZ8.3.P423Sl   [398.2]   [E]   78-55625
                         ISBN 0-03-044966-9

Weekly Reader Books' edition

Sleeping Beauty
with Benjy and Bubbles

Adapted by RUTH LERNER PERLE

Illustrated by GIULIO MAESTRO

Holt, Rinehart and Winston • New York

HR&W Books

In a distant country, far from here,
A King and Queen, one long ago year,
Lived all alone with only one care —
No child had come to answer their prayer.
The castle was silent with no sign of joy
And no shouts of glee from a girl or a boy.

Year after year, their great sadness grew
And none in the Kingdom knew what to do.
And when Benjy the bunny tried to cheer them,
They just wept when he came near them.

A King and Queen were sad.
They did not have a child.

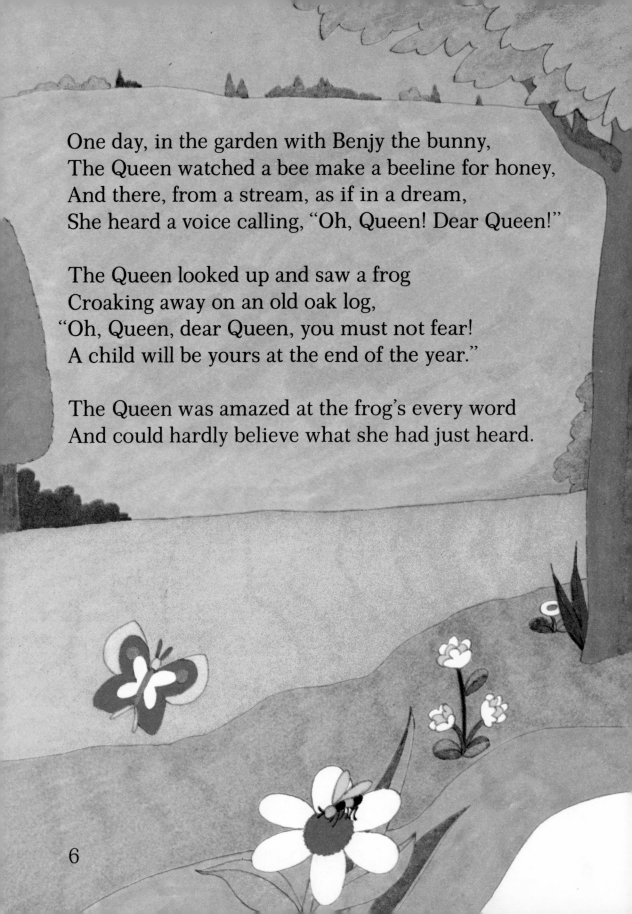

One day, in the garden with Benjy the bunny,
The Queen watched a bee make a beeline for honey,
And there, from a stream, as if in a dream,
She heard a voice calling, "Oh, Queen! Dear Queen!"

The Queen looked up and saw a frog
Croaking away on an old oak log,
"Oh, Queen, dear Queen, you must not fear!
A child will be yours at the end of the year."

The Queen was amazed at the frog's every word
And could hardly believe what she had just heard.

The Queen saw a frog.
"You will have a child soon,"
called the frog.

But as the frog promised, the next Christmas brought her
The gift of all gifts—a beautiful daughter
With raven black hair that shone in the sun,
Bright, smiling lips and eyes full of fun.
She looked like a flower blossoming wild,
So the Queen chose the name, Thorn Rose, for the child.

Soon the Queen had a little girl.
She was a beautiful Princess.

The King and the Queen planned a great celebration
And sent each of twelve Fairies an engraved invitation.
Then all the minstrels in the land
Came to play with the royal band.
They played all the tunes ever written and then
They played them over and over again.

Of course, the twelve Fairies who were invited
Came to the party and they were excited!
They laughed and sang and supped and sipped
And sang and swayed and bowed and dipped.

But Benjy hopped about in fright;
He knew of a Fairy they forgot to invite!
And *that was a terrible oversight!*

The King and Queen had a party.
They invited twelve fairies.
One fairy was not invited.

When the twelve good Fairies had wined and dined,
They gave Thorn Rose wishes—the best of each kind.
The first gave her beauty, the second, great wealth,
The third wished her virtue, the fourth wished her health;
And when the eleventh her wish had presented,
Lo! The uninvited Fairy entered.
Wildly, she flew about the room
With Bubbles the cat on an old-fashioned broom.

Then the fairy who was not invited came.
She was very angry.

The furious Fairy, with an eerie screech,
Unrolled an old scroll and started her speech:
"To the King and Queen, my greetings cold,
When Princess Thorn Rose is fifteen years old,
She'll follow the strains of a mysterious tune
And discover a spinning wheel in an old room;
She'll prick her thumb and fall in a swoon
And be a dead Princess by rise of the moon!

The curse, now cast, she mounted her broom,
Sweeping herself and the cat from the room.

The angry fairy said, "When the Princess is fifteen, she will see a spinning wheel. She will stick her finger. Then she will die."

The King and the Queen were struck spellbound
And sat in their thrones without making a sound.

Then the twelfth Fairy said, "*I* can alter that will!
Remember, I still have *my* wish to fulfill.
Though the curse we just heard cannot be undone,
My wish *can* be a softening one.
When the child pricks her thumb and falls in a swoon,
She'll *not* be dead by the rise of the moon!
Instead, she will sleep for a full hundred years
When a Prince will awake her with a kiss and a tear."

Then a good fairy said,
"The Princess will *not* die!
She will sleep for one hundred years.
Then a Prince will wake her.

The King and the Queen bade their fair guests farewell,
Then thought of the ways of preventing the spell
They agreed that Thorn Rose could not prick her hand
If all spinning wheels were removed from the land.
The King then commanded by royal decree
All spinning wheels thrown into the deep sea.

The King said, "The Princess must not stick her finger. We must get rid of all the spinning wheels."

Never again was a spinning wheel seen
In the Kingdom until Thorn Rose was fifteen.
Though all had forgotten the evil spell's power,
Poor Thorn Rose was fated to go to the tower.

On the day of her birthday, she skipped up the stair
And heard a wheel whirring, like a tune playing there.
She followed the sound to the top tower floor
And there, in the darkness, spied a half open door.

Soon the Princess was fifteen years old.
She went up to a little room.

Inside, sat a woman who cried, "Do come in!
Step in more closely and watch as I spin."

Thorn Rose was enchanted by the whirring machine,
The likes of which she never had seen.
She reached out to touch it and so, pricked her thumb
And in an instant her body was numb.
She fell in a swoon upon a small bed—
Not dead, but asleep, as the good Fairy had said.

Then Bubbles sprang up and over a chair
And chased little Benjy down the long stair.

A spinning wheel was in the room.
The Princess stuck her finger.
She fell asleep.

As soon as Thorn Rose fell asleep on the bed,
The rest of the palace stopped as if dead.
All at the palace fell in a trance —
The band as it played, the maid mending pants,
Two flies with their wings outspread in the hall,
The butcher boy bouncing his ball on the wall.
The jesters and tumblers froze upside down
And so did the smile on the face of a clown!
The cook fell asleep, the Queen and the King,
The lizards, the frogs and the toads—everything!
Even the clock stopped chiming its chime
And the only one waking was Old Father Time.

Everyone else fell asleep too.

And Father Time counted each year after year
While the tale of the spell was told far and near.
And many a Prince to prove daring and duty
Tried to rescue Thorn Rose, now called Sleeping Beauty.
But a forest had grown round the castle's high wall
And none could get through it—no one at all.

When a hundred years passed, a Prince came to see
If he could set Sleeping Beauty free.
As he rode through the forest, the hedges all cleared
And then just like magic, the castle appeared!
He leaped up the steps and quietly crept
To the room in the tower where sweet Thorn Rose slept.
When he saw Sleeping Beauty in her bed fast asleep,
He kissed her smooth cheek and started to weep.
She stirred when she felt the kiss and the tears
And opened her eyes after those many years!

The beautiful Princess slept
one hundred years.
She was called Sleeping Beauty.
Then a Prince came and woke her.

At that very moment, the whole castle stirred
And all the familiar old sounds could be heard.
The cook, once again, was rattling his kettles,
The flowers stood straight and unfolded their petals,
A blackbird awoke and stretched out its wing
Then the clown woke up too, and the Queen and the King.
The butcher boy's ball bounced before long,
The musicians and singers burst into song!
The clock whizzed and whirred to tune up its chimes
And the castle rejoiced as in the old times.
Benjy the bunny hippety hopped
As if the time had never stopped!

Everyone else woke up too.

They danced and they sang and ate a big cake,
For Thorn Rose, the beauty, at last was awake.
The palace halls echoed with music and laughter,
And they all lived happily forever after.

Everyone was happy.

THE END